Barbro Lindgren and Eva Eriksson

ROSA

Goes to Daycare

A Groundwood Book

Douglas & McIntyre

VANCOUVER TORONTO BUFFALO

Summer is over. The fields and forests are gone, and now there are just streets and cars everywhere.

When Rosa and her aunt go out for a walk, Rosa sits down on the sidewalk. Or she lies down and closes her eyes.

When they come home, her aunt has to pet her all the time, or else Rosa growls. Dogs aren't supposed to sit at home and growl all day.

So now Rosa is starting daycare!

First you go through a door, up a few stairs, and then you're there. The first few days her aunt is allowed to come because Rosa is shy and wants to run home right away. She thinks it's terrible to be with all those dogs she doesn't know. What if one of them wants to bite her?

But all the dogs are nice. Mean dogs aren't allowed at this daycare. Once a mean dog came and wanted to bite. It wasn't allowed to come anymore and now it sits at home being mean instead.

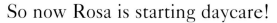

The dogs live in different rooms. The dachshund
Karo lives in Rosa's room. He likes girl dogs. That's why
there are only girl dogs in his room: Molly, Esther and
Rosa. Each dog has her own basket, and Karo takes
turns lying with each of them.

Every dog in the daycare has its own blanket, too.
And all the leashes hang on little hooks outside the door.

Haddock and Tuffy live in another room. Haddock is so happy and bouncy. But he has to be careful because he broke his leg when he was only a few weeks old. Poor Haddock. He has two hedgehogs and an old mitt to play with to help him cheer up.

Tuffy is really old and would rather not do anything all day. When Haddock gets too jumpy, Tuffy growls at him to calm down.

Charlie, Falco and Mysan live in one room. Mysan is shy—mostly with girl dogs, even though she's a girl herself.

Charlie and Falco are best friends. They are like two policemen who watch over everyone, so no one gets lost on walks. The other dogs don't see the point. They want to decide on their own whether they are going to get lost or not.

Jock, Rambo and Bobby live in the next room. Jock is scared of almost everything and only gets angry when someone takes his stick. Rambo is the smallest one in the whole daycare, but he thinks he's the biggest. He's even brave enough to scare German shepherds. On walks he wears a black turtleneck sweater. Sometimes Jock carries him by his sweater.

Bobby is like a bouncing ball. He jumps up and down all day. He'd like Rambo to jump, too. So instead he jumps right on top of Rambo.

Yellow Edwin and Dina live in the room closest to the entrance. They are brother and sister and pretty wild.

Then there's Grandma Miranda and Aunt Arielle. Aunt Arielle wants to decide everything, but Grandma always runs the show. And they wear such funny hats!

That's so their ears don't flop down into their food.

The first few days when Rosa goes for a walk, she lies
right down on the sidewalk and pretends she's dead.
The daycare ladies ask her aunt, "Does Rosa usually lie
down and pretend she's dead?"

"Yes, she does," says Rosa's aunt.

But after a week Rosa isn't as tired anymore. She starts walking faster. And one day the daycare ladies tell Rosa's aunt that something strange has happened. Rosa is no longer the last one when they go out. Now she's at the front with Falco and Charlie!

After their walk the dogs are supposed to sleep. Some lie in their own baskets. Some trade baskets with each other. A few cram themselves into one basket because it is so cozy.

Anyone who doesn't want to sleep has to sleep anyway. That's the way it is at daycare.

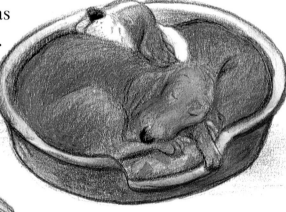

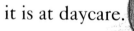

Rosa thinks it's more and more fun at daycare. One day she and Esther become best friends. Then Karo is sad, because he wants to be best friends with Rosa. But that won't work, because Esther is her best friend now. So Karo is her second-best friend, and Molly is her third-best friend.

Things are always happening at daycare. One day
Jock sits and scratches himself all over. When the
daycare ladies look closely, they see fleas crawling on
him! He has to go home right away to have a bath before
the fleas jump over to any of the other dogs.

The next day he comes back nice and clean.

Then Rosa gets a doggy cough. Dogs usually get one when they start daycare. Poor Rosa. Whenever she tries to bark, she coughs instead. She wonders why it sounds so funny. She doesn't know what a cough is.

Charlie and Jock are coughing, too. They don't understand why they sound so strange, either.

Sometimes one of the baskets is empty. That means a dog is on vacation. Right now Luddy is on vacation for a couple of days.

But Molly isn't. She's always busy, because she thinks she's having puppies. She lines her basket over and over again. Then she fetches balls and old socks to put in the basket. She pretends they're her babies. She even has a little fire engine for a baby.

Dogs get that way sometimes, but it passes. Rosa's doggy cough passes, too, so she can start barking again.

What doesn't pass is that Rosa still likes to suck on her blanket when she goes to sleep. The others think it's so babyish. They never suck on their blankets.

But Rosa can do something they can't do. She can do real somersaults!

The other dogs just stare. None of them can do somersaults.

Soon all the leaves have
fallen off the trees, and it gets
cold. One day big snowflakes come
tumbling through the air. This makes the daycare dogs
so happy. They roll in the snow and go sliding down the
hills. But Jock absolutely refuses to go. And Tuffy is too
old for sliding.

It snows for days. Suddenly there's ice where there used to be water. The dogs are surprised.

Where did the water go? And where did the ice come from?

Farther out a steamboat puffs along. It has broken its own path through the ice.

The dogs think it's so strange. They want to run out and look. But the daycare ladies won't let them.

"Don't run out onto the ice," they say. "Danger!"

The next day they see two men fishing far out on the ice. Rosa can see little fish lying next to holes in the ice.

Rosa likes fish. She wants to eat all the fish!

Now she's rushing out onto the ice!

"Stop, Rosa!" yell the daycare ladies. "Danger!"

Rosa doesn't stop. She runs as fast as she can.

"Stop, Rosa!" yell the ladies. "Stop!"

But Rosa can't stop. The ice is too slippery. She slides past the little fish out toward the watery path where the boats are, and—SPLASH!—she falls in the water.

The ladies are screaming. The dogs are barking and the water is totally black. Rosa is nowhere to be seen.

Then her surprised little face suddenly appears again.

The fishermen are there just in time. They grab Rosa by the ears and pull her up.

Rosa is so glad she has been saved. The ladies and the dogs come running. The fishermen give Rosa two little fish that she eats right away.

Then they have to rush back to the daycare, because Rosa is so cold that she is shaking. When they arrive, she gets to lie in Esther's basket. Esther lies down next to her on one side and Karo lies on the other side. And Molly squeezes in down by Rosa's feet. They lick her until she is completely dry. (It sounds strange, but it's actually true!)

Then she gets a cinnamon bun, and Esther and Karo and Molly each get one, too. And then they fall asleep.

At five Rosa's aunt comes to pick her up. The ladies
tell her about the little fish and the black water and how
Rosa fell in.

Then Rosa tells the story her way. She barks and barks
about how scared she was and how cold the water was. But
that then the fishermen pulled her up by the ears. And
then she got two little fish and they were so yummy!

Now she is happy. But she will never go in the water
again.

ROSA'S FRIENDS

KARO — brown dachshund

MOLLY — springer spaniel

ESTHER — Irish setter

HADDOCK — Saluki

TUFFY — cocker spaniel

CHARLIE — English spaniel

FALCO — Australian shepherd

MYSAN — all different kinds

JOCK — Munsterlander

RAMBO — miniature dachshund

BOBBY — standard poodle

YELLOW EDWIN — Afghan hound

DINA — Afghan hound

GRANDMA MIRANDA — Afghan hound

AUNT ARIELLE — Afghan hound

Text copyright © 1999 by Barbro Lindgren
Illustrations copyright © 1999 by Eva Eriksson
Translation copyright © 2000 by Maria Lundin

First published in the English language in Canada by
Groundwood Books 2000
Originally published in Sweden as *Rosa på dagis* by Eriksson &
Lindgren 1999

Groundwood Books / Douglas & McIntyre
720 Bathurst Street, Suite 500
Toronto, Ontario M5S 2R4

Distributed in the USA by Publishers Group West
1700 Fourth Street
Berkeley, CA 94710

We acknowledge the financial support of the Canada Council
for the Arts, the Ontario Arts Council and the Government of
Canada through the Book Publishing Industry Development
Program for our publishing activities.

Canadian Cataloguing in Publication Data

Lindgren, Barbro
Rosa goes to daycare
A Groundwood book. Translation of: Rosa på dagis.
ISNBN 0-88899-391-9
I. Eriksson, Eva. II. Title.
PZ7.L6585Rg 2000   j839.73'74   C00-93031-4

Printed and bound in Italy